MW01484531

Friendship
GROWS LIKE A GARDEN

LITTLE SIMON
New York   London   Toronto   Sydney

 LITTLE SIMON

An imprint of Simon & Schuster Children's Publishing Division

1230 Avenue of the Americas, New York, New York 10020

Holly Hobbie™ and related trademarks © 2006 Those Characters From Cleveland, Inc.

Used under license by Simon & Schuster, Inc. All rights reserved. American Greetings with
rose logo is a trademark of AGC, Inc.

Copyright © 2006 by Simon & Schuster, Inc.

Book designed by Aviva Presby

All rights reserved, including the right of reproduction in whole or in part in any form.

LITTLE SIMON is a registered trademark of Simon & Schuster, Inc., and associated
colophon is a trademark of Simon & Schuster, Inc.

Manufactured in Mexico

First Edition 10 9 8 7 6 5 4 3 2 1

ISBN-13: 978-1-4169-1779-3

ISBN-10: 1-4169-1779-9

This book is for:

_____

Given with love from:

_____

Love is good for growing things
whether large or small—
flowers, plants, and animals,
but friendships most of all!

Learn to share
and you will find
friendships of
the warmest kind.

A good friend has a special way
of making gray days bright,
by filling skies
with rays of sunshine
and gardens with colorful delight!

Friends who act with kindness
can brighten up the day,
adding sunshine with a smile
and the caring things they say.

Sharing the pleasures friendship brings
adds beauty to the simplest things,
like sunshine and showers
in the spring
make flowers bloom
and bluebirds sing.

Friendships grow more beautiful
with every passing day,
like a single flower blossoming
into a glorious bouquet.

When you water the seeds of friendship
with loyalty and care,
the buds that bloom
will fill your heart
and make happiness grow anywhere.

Spending days with friends so true,
laughing under skies so blue—
make all the world
seem bright and new
and bring joy to everything we do.

Friendships are like blooming flowers
wherever they appear,
in vibrant colors and scents so sweet,
spreading happiness and cheer.

Love is the gift we give with our hearts
to the dearest of our friends,
like a big bouquet of sunshine
glowing with warmth that never ends.

Laughter, smiles,
and memories—
friendships are made
with all of these.

HOLLY HOBBIE

The greatest friendships are for keeps
and last throughout the years—
through winter, summer,
spring, and fall,
through laughter, joy, and tears.

Friendships are gifts sent from above,
blessings granted to keep us warm
and give us hope
when days are dark—
like the rainbow after a storm.

When good friends
are far apart,
hearing from them
warms the heart.

Growing Friendship Flowers:

🌻 Plant your friendship anywhere you want happiness to bloom.

🌻 Shower the seeds with plenty of love.

🌻 Fertilize with fun.

🌻 Spread warmth evenly across the buds.

🌻 Bright bouquets of friendship will bloom throughout the year.